The

Fourth of July

A Level Two Reader

By Cynthia Klingel and Robert B. Noyed

The Child's World®

Ooooooh! Aaaaaah! It is time for the Fourth of July.

The Fourth of July is a special day in the United States. It began more than 200 years ago.

Long ago, on July 4, America became a free country. People still remember this freedom on July 4 each year.

7

Many people go on trips on the Fourth of July. They visit places that are important in America's history.

Many cities have parades on the Fourth of July. People stand along the streets to watch the marchers go by.

People wave flags. Red, white, and blue are the colors we see on the Fourth of July.

13

Colorful floats come down the street. Bands play, and music fills the air.

People have picnics and summer parties. It is a great time to see family and friends.

BOOM! BANG! At night, fireworks light up the sky. Fireworks are one of the best parts of the Fourth of July.

On the Fourth of July, people remember what it means to live in the United States. The Fourth of July is a day to be proud.

Index

To Find Out More

Books

Dalgliesh, Alice. *The 4th of July Story*. New York: Aladdin, 1995.

Merrick, Patrick. *Fourth of July Fireworks*. Chanhassen, Minn.: Child's World, 2000.

Ziefert, Harriet. *Hats Off for the Fourth of July*. New York: Penguin Putnam Books for Young Readers, 2000.

Web Sites

Celebrate! Holidays in the U.S.A.: Independence Day
http://www.usis.usemb.se/Holidays/celebrate/independ.html
For an article about the Fourth of July from a U.S. embassy.

Frequently Asked Questions about the Flag
http://www.legion.org/our_flag/of_faq_flag.htm
For information about the American flag from the American Legion.

Note to Parents and Educators

Welcome to Wonder Books®! These books provide text at three different levels for beginning readers to practice and strengthen their reading skills. Additionally, the use of nonfiction text provides readers the valuable opportunity to *read to learn*, not just to learn to read.

These leveled readers allow children to choose books at their level of reading confidence and performance. Nonfiction Level One books offer beginning readers simple language, word choice, and sentence structure as well as a word list. Nonfiction Level Two books feature slightly more difficult vocabulary, longer sentences, and longer total text. In the back of each Nonfiction Level Two book are an index and a list of books and Web sites for finding out more information. Nonfiction Level Three books continue to extend word choice and length of text. In the back of each Nonfiction Level Three book are a glossary, an index, and a list of books and Web sites for further research.

State and national standards in reading and language arts emphasize using nonfiction at all levels of reading development. Wonder Books® fill the historical void in nonfiction material for primary grade readers with the additional benefit of a leveled text.

About the Authors

Cynthia Klingel has worked as a high school English teacher and an elementary school teacher. She is currently the curriculum director for a Minnesota school district. Cynthia lives with her family in Mankato, Minnesota.

Robert B. Noyed started his career as a newspaper reporter. Since then, he has worked in school communications and public relations at the state and national level. Robert lives with his family in Brooklyn Center, Minnesota.

Published by The Child's World®, Inc.
PO Box 326
Chanhassen, MN 55317-0326
800-599-READ
www.childsworld.com

Photo Credits
© Art Montes de Oca/FPG International: 13
© Jean Higgins/Unicorn Stock Photos: 14
© 2000 Joseph Kayne/Dembinsky Photo Assoc. Inc.: 6
© Myrleen Ferguson Cate/PhotoEdit: 21
© North Wind Pictures: 5
© Paul Conklin/PhotoEdit: 9
© 2003 Robert E. Daemmrich/Stone: 18
© Robin Rudd/Unicorn Stock Photos: 17
© Romie Flanagan: cover
© 2003 Ron Sherman/Stone: 10
© 2003 William S. Heisel/Stone: 2

Project Coordination: Editorial Directions, Inc.
Photo Research: Alice K. Flanagan

Library of Congress Cataloging-in-Publication Data
Klingel, Cynthia Fitterer.
The Fourth of July / by Cynthia Klingel and Robert B. Noyed.
    p. cm.
Includes bibliographical references and index.
ISBN 1-56766-954-9 (lib. bdg. : alk. paper)
1. Fourth of July—Juvenile literature.
2. Fourth of July celebrations—Juvenile literature.
[1. Fourth of July. 2. Holidays.] I. Noyed, Robert B. II. Title.
E286 .A1385 2001
394.2634—dc21

                    00-011361